BARNEY SALTZBERG

Would You Rather be a Princess or a Dragon?

A NEAL PORTER BOOK
ROARING BROOK PRESS
NEW YORK

Would you rather be a
princess or a dragon?
You'll never know which one
to be until you've tried.

If you want to be a princess
or a dragon, here's a book
that might help you decide.

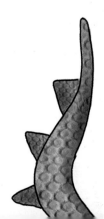

If you want to be a princess . . .

you should wear a lot of pink.

If you want to be
a dragon . . .

being green would help, I think.

If you want to be a princess
practice walking straight and tall.

If you want to be a dragon
practice bouncing off the wall.

A princess loves her bubble baths.

A dragon never bathes.

A princess is polite.

A dragon misbehaves.

When a princess eats her food
she takes a teeny, tiny bite.

A dragon on the other hand
eats everything in sight.

A princess likes to practice her perfect princess wave.

A dragon likes to look for the perfect dragon cave.

A princess loves to smile in a dainty princess way.

A dragon is just wild,
being dragony all day.

From time to time a princess
needs to take a little break.

There is only so much pink that even princesses can take.

Sometimes a little
princess wants
to be a little wild.

Because inside every princess
is a little dragon child.

And inside every dragon,
I can say without a doubt . . .

there's a little princess . . .

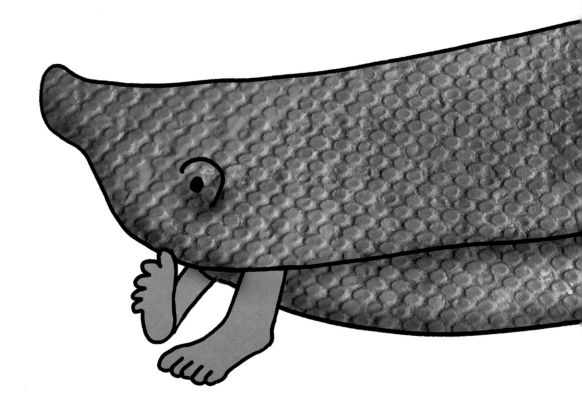

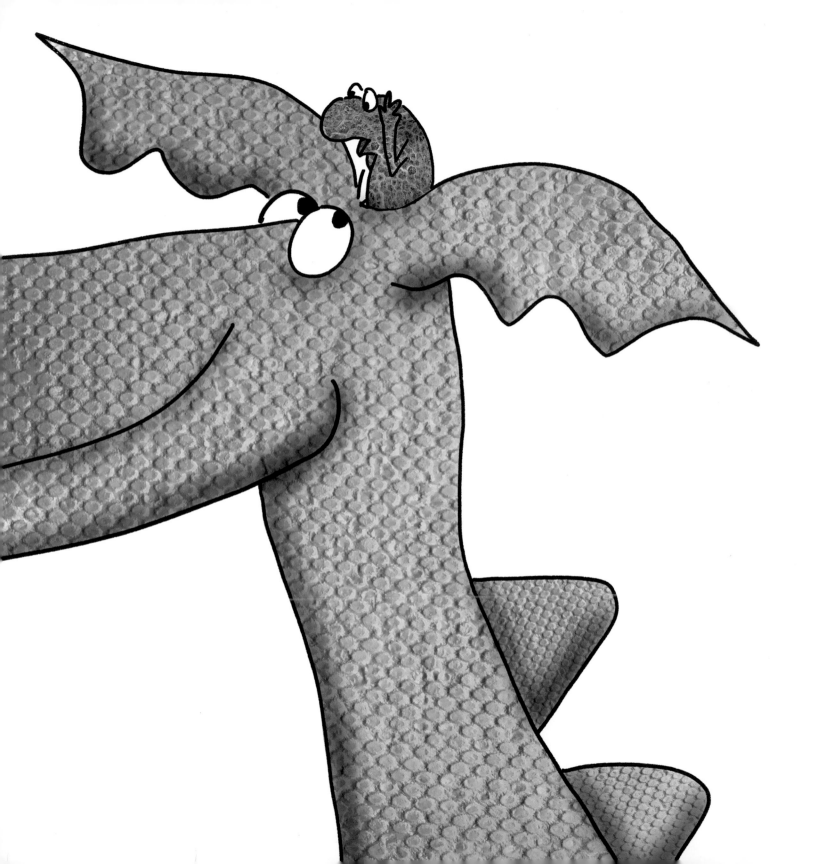

waiting . . .

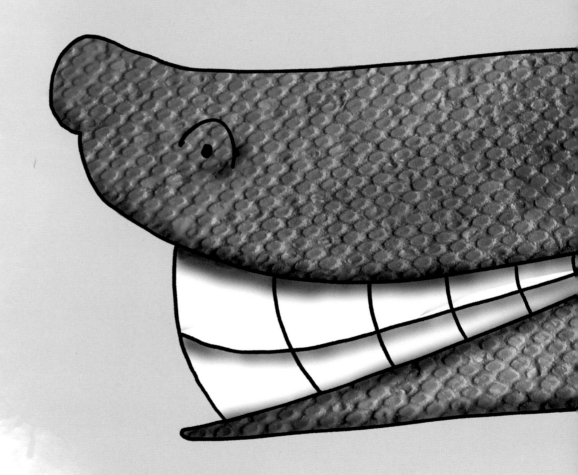

to come out.

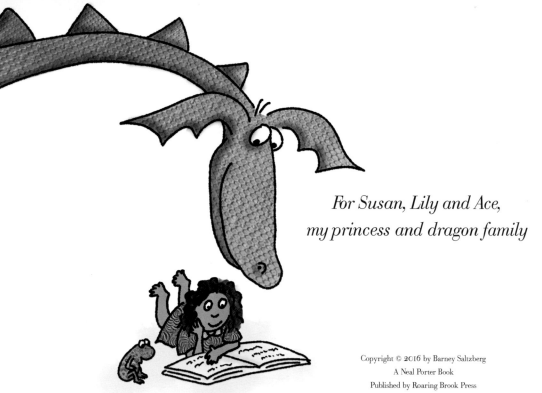

For Susan, Lily and Ace,
my princess and dragon family

Copyright © 2016 by Barney Saltzberg

A Neal Porter Book

Published by Roaring Brook Press

Roaring Brook Press is a division of Holtzbrinck Publishing Holdings Limited Partnership

175 Fifth Avenue, New York, New York 10010

The art for this book was collaged digitally using paint, paper, and wire.

mackids.com

Library of Congress Congress Cataloging-in-Publication Data

Names: Saltzberg, Barney, author, illustrator.

Title: Would you rather be a princess or a dragon? / Barney Saltzberg.

Description: First edition. | NewYork : Roaring Brook Press, 2016. | "A Neal
    Porter Book." | Summary: "Some little ones want to be princesses; others
    want to be dragons. The message of this book is that you can actually be
    both! There are lots of things you can be: a little wild, a little sweet.
    A little polite, a little troublesome. A little dainty, a little
    dragony"— Provided by publisher.

Identifiers: LCCN 2015042496 | ISBN 9781626723580 (hardback)

Subjects: | CYAC: Stories in rhyme. | Princesses—Fiction. | Dragons—Fiction. |
    BISAC: JUVENILE FICTION / Animals / Mythical. | JUVENILE FICTION /
    Concepts / Opposites. | JUVENILE FICTION / Fairy Tales & Folklore / General.

Classification: LCC PZ8.3.S174 Wo 2016 | DDC [E]—dc23

LC record available at http://lccn.loc.gov/2015042496

Our books may be purchased in bulk for promotional, educational, or business use. Please
contact your local bookseller or the Macmillan Corporate and Premium Sales Department
at (800) 221-7945 ext. 5442 or by e-mail at MacmillanSpecialMarkets@macmillan.com.

First edition 2016

Printed in China by Toppan Leefung Printing Ltd., Dongguan City, Guangdong Province

1 3 5 7 9 10 8 6 4 2